Be sure to look for all the great McGee and Me books and videos at your favorite bookstore.

Focus on the Family

PRESENTS

The Big Lie

Bill Myers and Ken Johnson

Tyndale House Publishers, Inc.
Wheaton, Illinois

Front cover illustration by Morgan Weistling
Interior illustrations by Nathan Greene

Library of Congress Catalog Card Number 89-50275
ISBN 0-8423-4169-2

McGee & Me is a trademark of Living Bibles International
Copyright 1989 by Living Bibles International
Printed in the United States of America
2 3 4 5 6 7 8 9 10 95 94 93 92 91 90 89

Contents

ONE
Beginnings . . .

I pulled my space shooter from its holster. Time was running out. I had to reach my aircraft. The planet beneath me was about to go to pieces.

Just ahead of me lay a dark hallway filled with smoke. Live electric cables flipped wildly across my path. One touch from them meant total destruction— and that would mean no pizza for a long, long time.

Taking a deep breath I leaped into the hall. The first cable hissed and crackled just over my head. I hurdled another cable, then another, and another. Finally the exit hatch lay just in front of me.

I stretched my hand toward the release handle. But a green slimy tentacle suddenly wrapped itself around my wrist. One of the guards must have hidden himself in the darkness.

"Prepare yourself for the worst," he gurgled.

"Hah!" I laughed, turning to face him. "I've already had lima beans in cream gravy. . . . Your threats don't scare me!"

But even as I spoke, another oozing tentacle curled around my throat. He pulled me off my feet and lurched forward. His face was hideous. And his wicked smile showed grimy teeth that had never seen a dentist.

I knew in a few more seconds I'd be dead. So I brought my space shooter up with lightning speed. "I've got no time to dance, frog-face," I sputtered through his choke hold. A blast exploded from my laser and consumed the green goon.

A rumbling sound below reminded me that my time was almost up. I had to get off this planet. I quickly bounded through the exit hatch. I reached the planet's surface and made for my aircraft.

As I leaped into the cockpit, the ground opened up in front of me. Fire shot up from the inside of this lost and dying world.

I hit the ignition. A bolt of fear shot through me as my engine coughed and sputtered. I didn't have any jumper cables so I did what any good mechanic would do—I kicked the control panel. The engine roared to life!

I engaged the lifters and blasted into the star-filled sky.

As I reached orbit, the planet below exploded. A million meteors shot into the sky. I settled back for the trip home, satisfied. The formula for low-fat, freeze-dried pickles was tucked securely in my space jacket. The world would again be a safer, if not thinner, place to live.

Pretty exciting stuff, huh? But, believe it or not, that adventure was nothing compared to the one Nick and I were about to take. But I guess I'm getting a little ahead of myself.

My name is McGee. I came about through the talents and imagination of my best buddy, Nicholas Martin. You see, at the ripe old age of eleven, Nick is what you'd call a cartoonist. And we've been together from the first day he drew my adorable image on his sketch pad. And we stay together for good reasons. Sure, it's Nick who imagines and draws my amazing escapes (like the one I just mentioned). But it's me who makes sure my shy little pal finds the adventures in real life.

Adventures like those first few days at the new school—back when we all moved into Grandma Martin's house. And by "all" I'm talking about the WHOLE family. . . .

First, there's Nick's older sister Sarah. She's an OK kid, I guess—except she likes to give orders and mess with her hair a lot.

Then there's his kid sister Jamie—a real cutie with a permanent ring of jelly around her mouth.

As for Grandma, she's my kind of gal . . . spunky, full of energy. In fact, she even spent a few years as a missionary. I don't know how old she is, but rumor has it she helped Ben Franklin put the tail on his kite.

Then there's Nick's father, or "Mr. Dad" as I call him. He's a swell guy . . . honest, funny. And does he know his Bible? Let me tell you, Billy Graham's got nothing over this guy. He works as managing editor at the local newspaper, which gives me and Nick plenty of chances to get information to help solve crimes and stuff.

Then there's Mom. Like Grandma, she's smart as a whip and spends lots of time helping people who have needs. She also makes great pancakes.

Lastly, and most certainly least, there is a creature so awful words cannot describe him. In fact, his name says it all—"Whatever." As the family dog, I think he's a cross between a Pekingese and a Poodle. I'm not sure, but it comes out ugly anyway you look at it. Besides, he sheds.

Anyway, about that adventure. It's probably best if I let you read it on your own. But don't worry, I'll be dropping in from time to time to make sure you get the facts straight—especially about the role I played in this, one of our greatest adventures.

It was six months ago that Mom and Dad had asked the family to think about moving in with Grandma. Everyone was pretty excited. The kids had always loved the old house with its mysterious past. They loved the cellar. They loved the attic. And best of all they loved checking the loose bricks for hidden treasure and tapping the walls for secret passageways. So far, no luck. But that wouldn't stop them from trying.

Mom and Dad had other reasons for the move . . .

First of all there was Grandma. As much as she hated to admit it, she was definitely getting older and those stairs were definitely getting steeper.

Then there was the fact that Dad wanted to get the children out of the suburbs. It seemed that all that money and all that snobbery was starting to have an effect on the kids. "Half the world is starving to death," he said. "And the only thing our neighbors care about is who gives the best tennis lessons." Dad wanted the kids to be with real people who had real needs. "Let's put our faith into action," he said. "Let's see how we can help."

And finally there was Mom. Instead of her hectic teaching job, she felt that she should be spending more time with her family. "The kids won't be kids forever," she said. "I just want to be around in case they need me."

So . . .

Mom quit her job at the Junior College.

Dad left his job as assistant editor at *The Tribune* and took over the small community paper.

And Grandma now had the entire family living with her.

Everything was perfect. Except for one small detail . . . no one bothered to tell the kids how different life would be in the city.

Nicholas began to suspect it when his bike was stolen. It had barely made it off the moving van before it was gone.

And Sarah began to suspect it when she discovered that the nearest mall was almost ten miles away.

But that was only the beginning. . . .

Monday was hectic. Grandma's kitchen hadn't seen such activity in years. The Martin children and Mom and Dad were squeezing past each other. They were climbing over and around dozens of unpacked boxes.

"Where's my blue denim coat?" Sarah demanded. "Has anybody seen my blue denim coat?"

But no one was paying much attention. Mrs. Martin was hunting for bugs with a fly swatter the size of Kansas. Grandma was reminding everyone that the fire in the toaster had started out as bread. Mr. Martin was doing his best imitation of a handyman as he tried to fix the broken paper-towel rack. And little Jamie was sitting on top of the tallest stack of boxes, quietly munching the last of the Captain Crunch.

At last Nicholas himself came into the room. And by the look on his face it was pretty easy to see that he hadn't quite been able to "rise and shine" that morning.

"Hurry, honey. You don't want to be late for your first day at school," Mom said.

Being late wasn't exactly what Nick had in mind. More like never showing up. With eyes sealed shut, he somehow managed to fumble for the nearest box of cereal and dump it into a bowl.

"Please God," he was praying, "don't let it be bran."

"There, solid as a rock," Dad said as he gave the paper-towel holder a proud pat.

Nicholas paid little attention. He was thinking about his chances of survival at the new school.

Meanwhile, the dog had hopped up on one of the nearby boxes and started gobbling down somebody's toast.

"Get down from there," Dad shouted at the dog.

He scampered off. But Sarah, who had her back to the whole thing, spun around to her pet's defense.

"Daddy, why are you always picking on Whatever?"

Her father opened his mouth to explain. But Sarah, who was too busy being a teenager, cut him off. "Honestly, Daddy, you've got to learn to loosen up."

With that she popped the remainder of the dog-chewed toast in her mouth.

Dad started to warn her but caught himself. "You're right, honey," was all he said. "I'll try harder." He caught Nicholas's eye and gave him a little wink. Nick managed to smile back.

The phone began to ring and Grandma headed off to answer it. Meanwhile, Sarah, in a last-ditch effort, turned to her little sister. "Jamie, have *you* seen my blue denim coat?"

The girl nodded and Sarah's face lit up.

"You have? Where?"

"I was with you the day you bought it."

The light faded as quickly as it was lit. And, with the world's longest sigh, Sarah turned back out of the kitchen to continue her search.

Jamie quietly followed.

"Look at the time," Dad said, as he glanced at his watch. "I was supposed to be at the paper by 7:30." He gave Mom a quick peck on the cheek and was out the door with the usual good-byes.

Meanwhile, Sarah was calling for help in her search and rescue efforts from the other room. "Mother, *please* . . . MOTHER!"

"Coming!" Mom called as she reached for a paper towel and suddenly wound up with the entire "solid-as-a-rock" towel holder in her hand. She groaned slightly as she headed out the room.

Now, at last, Nicholas was alone. Now, at last, he could have some peace. Now, at last, he could have some quiet. Or so he thought . . .

TWO
Breakfast Adventures

I tried to adjust my eyes to the darkness around me. But it was of no use. I was going to have to feel my way along the jagged walls around me. I was trying to find the famous Eye of Darryl Jewel. I would've said things looked hopeless but it was so dark in there I couldn't tell how things looked!

Suddenly, the cave rocked violently. Loose stones and boulders fell from above. I darted back and forth, dodging one after another after another —a neat trick in the dark.

Finally things started to settle down. I was beginning to feel kind of pleased with myself, having survived another cave-in. But it wasn't over yet.

I heard a low rumbling from behind. I spun around just in time to see a huge boulder rolling right toward me! I tried to hurry out of the way but the walls of the cave were so narrow that there was no place for me to hide. The boulder crashed into me and knocked me to the ground. I hit my head and passed out.

When I awoke I noticed that the cave-in had dislodged just enough rocks from above to allow a small shaft of light to pour into my cramped quarters. I could see!

I could see, all right. I could see my legs were pinned behind my old pal, the boulder. I could see that I had really gotten myself in a fix this time. And for what? A jewel?

Ah, yes . . . the jewel. I had to get that jewel. Lying around the cave wasn't getting it done. So, in one swift move I placed my hands against the rock's bumpy surface and pushed. A loud groan echoed in the cave. The noise continued to grow as I pushed harder and harder. It must have been about two minutes before I realized the groan was coming from me.

All that work and the boulder hadn't moved an inch. Well, I sort of liked it here anyway. Hang some pictures, maybe some curtains—it wouldn't be so bad.

Yeah, right, and sticking your tongue in a blender only tickles.

I had to find a solution. Or, maybe, a solution was about to find me. Because, once again, the cave began to shake. Only this time it was more gentle— more like vibrations. And, as the boulder began to vibrate, I was able to squirm, wiggle, and inch my legs out from under it. The dust and tiny rocks from above kept falling and bouncing off my head. I couldn't help wondering, "Is this what eggs feel like when we salt and pepper them?"

At last, I freed my feet and rolled aside . . . just as a huge rock crashed down exactly where my head had been. Nick says I'm hard-headed, but I'm glad I hadn't stuck around to find out.

Slowly the shaking began to stop and everything was quiet. . . . Yep, you guessed it, too quiet. I couldn't hear a thing.

I snapped my fingers . . . nothing.

I clapped my hands . . . still nothing!

This was just plain crazy. What kind of place was this, anyway?

Suddenly, I felt a tickle in my ear. I shook my head and a half cup of dirt, two stones, and a moth named Felix came out of my ears. I could hear again! What a relief to know they had only been plugged. I'd still be able to enjoy listening to myself sing in the shower.

I moved on carefully, my way still dimly lit from the shaft of light above. Up ahead I thought I saw a faint glow. Was it just another light shaft, or could it be the prize I was seeking, the wonderful Eye of Darryl Jewel? Who knows? With thoughts like these racing through my mind I began to worry that maybe those "little" rocks that hit me on the head hadn't been so little after all.

In any case, as I worked my way toward the glow I began to recall the stories and fables told of the ancient jewel—its incredible beauty and untold worth. Soon it would be mine—all mine! Of course I'd be generous and share it with all the little people who had so feebly tried to help me along the way. . . . Come to think of it, I don't know anybody "littler" than me. Oh well, I guess I'll just have to cope with all that wealth by myself.

By now the glorious glow was just a few yards

ahead. This was no shaft of light. This was the moment I had dreamed about!

Closer . . . closer . . . closer . . .

There, at last. It was right in front of me. I could see it clearly now. It was beyond description! It was unlike anything I had dreamed of! It was a . . . a . . . magnifying glass! A magnifying glass? Yeah, it was just a magnifying glass, all right.

So much for legends and fables. Here, I had risked my life and limb—and for what? For some cheap little toy that made things look bigger. And now, as I held it up, I realized it made everything look bigger—even my stupidity.

But I had no time to dwell on IQs. Because, just at that moment, I heard scraping and clawing. It was coming from below and it was making its way toward me . . . loud and fast. . . loud and fast. I figured now was as good a time as any to start picking up my pace. I mean, I didn't want to hang around all day. I had things to do, people to see, and spooky things that climb in caves to run away from! It wasn't that I was scared or anything like that. It's just that it suddenly occurred to me I might have left my electric train running back at the sketch pad.

So I began to climb . . . fast.

But the faster I climbed the faster it climbed. The clawing and grunting sounds grew louder by the second. I was concerned about it catching up. Slipping and falling back into the pit to face "The Guardian of the Magnifying Glass" was not my idea of a good time.

I kept climbing as fast as I could. But I knew I

couldn't keep up the pace much longer. I was about to blow a lung. Something had to give. And, as fate would have it, something did. . . .

As I placed my foot on a large rock, it gave way beneath me. I started falling. But, at the last second, I managed to grab a small opening in the stony wall. I held on for dear life, expecting the monster to be on top of me any second. But I never saw him. Instead, all I heard was the dull thud of the large rock on what must have been the monster's head. Then I heard the tumbling and bouncing sound as both of them fell into the darkness below.

Moments later I made my way to the opening of the cave, coughing and sputtering from the dust of my adventure.

Much to my surprise, my little buddy, Nick, was there to greet me. And, not wanting to alarm him, I casually lifted my magnifying glass to one eye and calmly exclaimed, "Here's looking at you, kid."

"What are you doing?" he replied.

I figured he was trying not to show his concern.

Now, it's true, the "cave" did look a lot like his breakfast cereal box . . . and, OK, so maybe the magnifying glass was just the prize in that box. But at least he could congratulate me for my great imagination and for a job well done. I mean, I did get the prize.

But I could see he had other things on his mind. Most of them having to do with the move to the new neighborhood . . . and to the new school.

"First day at a new school, huh, kid?" I said.

"Yeah," he mumbled as he took another bite of his cereal.

"Ah, cheer up. It's like I always say," I began as I

hopped out of the cereal box and onto the table, "make a big first impression and the rest is a piece of cake." I have a lot of catchy sayings like that but it didn't seem to faze ol' Nick. Not today.

"Right, McGee," he said. "Remember the last time you told me to make a big impression?"

"Sure, at the All-School Play." I also have a great memory.

"Yeah, you told me to push my way to the front of the stage so everybody could see me."

"Right," I agreed. "You were a smash!"

"Sure, when I fell over the edge into Bobby Rusco's tuba!"

"Well, at least you made an impression," I joked. But Nick wasn't laughing.

Mom called from the other room. "Hurry, Nicholas, or you'll be late for school."

With magnifying glass still in hand, I strolled over to my sketch pad lying on the table. Nicholas called back, "Right, Mom."

Scooping up his backpack, he reached for the pad only to find me poised in my best Sherlock Holmes outfit, peering through my new-found prize. "Nice, huh?" I grinned, hoping it would add a little cheer to his life.

"Grow up," was all he said as he slammed the pad shut.

It was going to be a long day. . . .

THREE
Tough Times for the New Kid

School was worse than Nick had imagined. Being the "new kid" was one thing. But being the new kid and looking like a total dweeb was a whole 'nother ball game—a game that Nicholas had become a star player in by the end of the day.

First there was the matter of finding his room. A simple task, right? The office wrote down the number 19 on a piece of paper and gave it to him. The only problem was they gave it to him upside down. So, as the bell rang and everyone ran to their rooms, poor Nicholas was still searching for room 61 instead of 19. The job was made even tougher since the room numbers only went up to 21.

By the time the tardy bell rang, all the kids had slipped into their classes. All except Nicholas, that is. Now he was alone in the hall. There was no one to ask for help. Nicholas grew more and more desperate as he kept searching for a room that didn't exist . . . until suddenly, out of nowhere, Coach Slayter appeared.

Now, at last, there was help.

Well, not exactly. If it had been any other teacher except Slayter, Nick would have been right. But it was Slayter, so he was wrong.

The coach was probably an OK guy—down deep inside, *way* down inside, so far down that nobody saw it. Basically, the man only had one problem. It had to do with kids. He hated them. Well, not really *hate.* He just thought that all kids were headed for trouble.

For this reason the kids did everything they could to stay out of his way. It's true, they had to sit through his health class. And it's true, they had to put up with his drill-sergeant-type yelling every Tuesday and Thursday when he came over from the middle school to teach P.E. But nobody, *nobody* ever made the mistake of crossing him.

Well, almost nobody. . . .

Nicholas swallowed hard as he slowly looked up—past the huge thighs, past the bulging stomach, and finally to the neckless head.

"A little soon to be cutting class, isn't it, mister?"

Nicholas gave a frail grin and tried to swallow. But of course there was nothing to swallow. His mouth was as dry as cotton. And before he could explain that he could not find room 61 . . . before he could explain that he was brand new, Slayter had him by the collar and was dragging him back toward the office. Another trouble-maker was busted.

Then there was lunch . . .

All the kids were hanging around the room, busy being kids—laughing, talking, having good times.

Nick had met a few of them. But most of them were too caught up in their little groups to pay him much attention. That is, until he carried his knapsack over to the coat racks and got his lunch. It was a simple procedure, right? I mean anyone could toss his knapsack up on the shelf and grab his lunch, right? But not today. Not for Nick. Not the way his luck was running.

He tossed the knapsack up on the shelf. But the shelf was a little higher than he thought. The knapsack came tumbling back down—right in his face. No biggie. Could happen to anyone. He tossed it up again. Again it fell. And again. And, well you guessed it. Then he heard it . . . giggling.

He glanced over his shoulder to see two girls. They were sitting on nearby desks and covering their mouths. There were no sounds now. But their bodies were shaking and their eyes crinkling. It was a safe guess that they were the ones who had been enjoying his show.

Nick recognized the one girl right away. She was wearing a silver bow in her hair. "It looks like something from my Erector set," Nick had thought while staring at it a few classes earlier. The rest of her outfit was as equally weird. A bright pink coat with big black spots. Matching zebra sunglasses that she twirled around and around in her hand. And a zillion bracelets that clanged and tinkled every time she moved—something she did a lot of.

Nicholas felt the edges of his ears start to burn. He wasn't used to being such a moron. He tried to cover up by giving the girls a weak little smile. Then, one last time, he gave the knapsack a mighty heave. Finally, *finally* it stayed put. Success!

He looked back to the girls and gave a little chuckle as he reached for his sack lunch. Now he was in control. Now he could laugh at himself with the best of them. After all, he was definitely not the clumsy fool they thought they were watching. He knew it. And now, by laughing at himself, they knew he knew it.

But, in his cool hipness, Nicholas grabbed his lunch sack by the wrong end. And, as he pulled it off the shelf, everything spilled out of the top—everything . . . his bologna sandwich, his Fritos, his Oreos, and his apple . . . which started rolling across the room.

The rest of the kids stopped talking and turned to watch the apple as it continued to roll. In the new silence it sounded like thunder. Finally, one person started to clap. Another followed and another . . . until the whole room was clapping . . . and laughing. Nicholas wasn't sure what to do. But the smile had worked before so he tried it again.

So there he was, trying to look like a good sport by wearing the stupidest grin he had ever worn in his life. His lunch lay all over the ground at his feet. Yes siree, if there were any doubts before, he put them all to rest. He definitely looked like the class idiot now.

Then there was recess . . .

Nicholas had been trying to decide whether or not he should go back into the classroom and get his sketch pad. Things had been pretty rough. To do a little drawing right now might cheer him up.

Maybe he could even have a little chat with McGee. But that last thought made him nervous. All he needed was for McGee to get out of hand and start acting up.

But Nicholas didn't need McGee to get him in trouble. Not just yet. Because, suddenly, he heard a whistle blow and a familiar voice yell out, "Hey you kids, come back here!"

Three kids rounded the corner of the building and ran head on into Nicholas. These guys were definitely in a hurry—no greetings, no apologies, not even a curse or two for him getting in their way. Instead, as they untangled themselves, each shoved a small can of something into his hands and was off.

Nicholas looked down at the cans he was now holding. They were different colors of spray paint. He thought it odd that the boys would give him such things. That is, until he finished rounding the corner and saw Coach Slayter with the whistle in his hand. The coach was not smiling.

For a moment Nick was confused . . . until he noticed the picture of the coach freshly painted on the wall beside the man.

Nicholas looked to the cans in his hands, then up to the coach.

He tried to smile.

Once again, Slayter grabbed him by the collar. Once again, the two were heading for the office.

Bang! clittery-clank-clank-clitter.
It wasn't the toughest day Nicholas ever had.
Bang! clank, clitter-clitter-clitter.

But at that moment he couldn't think of any that had been tougher.

Bang! clittery-clittery-clank.

"Make an impression," McGee had said. "Let everyone know who you are."

Well he had certainly done that. It's pretty hard to sit in the principal's office for half an hour writing "I will respect public property" a billion times. It's pretty hard to sit there as every teacher in school comes to check their box and looks down at you thinking, "Hmmm, another tough kid. Better keep my eye on him." It's pretty hard to do all that and *not* make an impression.

Bang! clittery-clank-clank-clitter.

Now, he was walking down an alley. A poor tomato juice can, whose label had worn off blocks ago, was taking the brunt of all his anger.

What else could possibly go wrong?

Bang! clittery-clank-clank . . . THUD.

He looked up.

Ahead of him were four boys standing in a circle. Citizens of the Month they were not. Long hair, pierced ears, dark sweatshirts. Let's just say they were the type of kids Coach Slayter hated. And, speaking of Slayter, suddenly it wouldn't have been so bad to have him around again. In fact, right now Nicholas wouldn't even have minded being in trouble again. . . . Especially as he looked helplessly at the four gang members glaring at him.

And the reason for the glare?

Nicholas's can was leaning against one of their skateboards.

"What do you think you're doin'?" the tallest member asked. His voice sounded hoarse and grave, like he'd just been munching on rocks. He probably had.

"Me?" Nicholas said. It was a stupid response but he couldn't think of anything smarter.

"Come here."

Nick hesitated but decided to obey—or at least his feet did. Getting closer to the gang was not what the rest of his body had in mind.

"Look at my skateboard," the thug said as he picked up the road-worn board. It was plastered from head to toe with heavy-metal decals. "You almost put a nick in it. What's your name?"

"Nick."

"Yeah, right, that's what I'm talkin' 'bout. Now what's your name, squid?"

". . . uh . . . Nick."

A couple of the gang members snickered. The leader threw them a look. Turning back to Nicholas, he grabbed the boy's shirt and pulled him in. "Oh, you're a funny man. A regular—"

Finally Nicholas caught on and quickly blurted out, "Nicholas . . . my name is Nicholas!"

The leader relaxed slightly. Apparently this new kid wasn't trying to be a smart-alec. He was just stupid.

"OK, St. Nicholas," the leader growled as the tiniest trace of a smile—or was it a sneer?—crossed his lips. "You got a present for me?"

"What?" Nick asked.

The anger started to return to the leader's voice. "If you come down my alley throwing cans at me,

29

you had better have some kind a peace offering."

Nicholas couldn't have been more lost. Getting a broken face was not his idea of a good time, but he had no idea what the leader was talking about.

"Money, stupid."

Glancing down and seeing the leader's right hand tightening into a fist, Nicholas knew two things. One, he had no money. And, two, that was the last answer in the world the kid wanted to hear.

"Well . . . I . . . uh," he stammered.

"Man, you're one lucky dude, kid."

The voice came from behind. Nicholas glanced out the corner of his eye for a better view.

"Beat it, Louis," the leader ordered.

But the kid kept approaching. He was black, Nicholas's age, and about half the leader's size.

"Sure man, but I just want him to realize what an honor it is to be beaten up by somebody like you."

Being honored was not exactly how Nicholas saw the situation—but he was grateful for any delay.

Louis continued, this time talking directly to Nick about the leader. "I bet you don't even know that this guy is the most roughest, baddest dude in the whole neighborhood. I mean he normally stomps guys twice your size."

Somehow, Nicholas didn't find that fact too comforting.

"But he's willing to risk his reputation by beating up somebody as wimpy as you. I mean my little sister could beat you up." He turned to the leader. "Ain't that right, Derrick?"

Derrick hesitated, unsure about how to respond.

"Go ahead," Louis encouraged. "Smash his face in."

Things were getting pretty muddy in the leader's mind. But smashing faces was one thing he understood. So, raising his fist, he prepared to do just that.

Nicholas closed his eyes, waiting for the worst. But, Louis wasn't finished. "I mean, people aren't going to fear him like they used to. His reputation will never be the same. But Derrick Cryder, a man of principle, is going to sacrifice all that on a little nothing like you."

Louis's logic began to make some kind of strange sense—at least to Derrick. And, after another moment of thought, the leader let Nicholas go with a shove. "Don't you wish," he said. But with the threat of bodily injury still very much on his mind, he growled, "I'm not going to forget you, squid. You either, Louis."

And with that, he turned and left. The rest of the gang followed.

"Hey, I'm your man," Louis called after him.

Now the two boys stood in silence for a moment. Nick's head was reeling over the slickness he had just seen. Talk about smooth. This kid was a work of art. In just two short minutes the little guy had turned the whole slug-fest around. Not only had he saved Nick's face, but he even managed to protect his own. All this without raising a fist. Incredible.

"Thanks, uh . . . " Nicholas was searching for his name.

"Louis," the boy said. And shrugging he added, "Forget it man."

With that the two turned and started down the alley. Neither knew it then, but a friendship was definitely in the making.

But the day's adventures were not over yet. Not by a long shot. . . .

FOUR
The Indian

Nicholas and Louis came around the corner and started up the street. Nick said good-bye to the boy and turned to cut across the neighbor's yard. He just lived a block over. By crossing through the driveway and into the next alley he'd be home in seconds.

But not this time.

"What are you doing?" Louis called.

A little taken by his tone, Nicholas stuttered, "I, uh, I was going home."

"Not that way you don't."

"Sure, I just live over on the other side. . . ."

"Man, what are you thinking? No one cuts across *that* yard."

"Why not?" Nicholas asked as he turned to look at the house. Now it's true, the house *did* seem a little spooky. . . . Three stories tall, broken shutters, pitch black windows, sagging roof. All right, it looked a *lot* spooky.

"He's a crazy Indian, man. He eats live animals.

They say anything that goes into that yard don't come out again!"

Nicholas could only stare. "What do you mean? Like pets and stuff?"

"Anything."

Enough said. Nick already had had enough adventure for the day—or even for the whole year. No way did he want to be eaten alive by some crazy man. But as he turned back to join Louis, he felt a sudden movement inside the art pad he was carrying. . . .

"Psst. Nick . . . Nick!" I was whispering, trying not to let Louis overhear. This was a perfect situation. I didn't want my little buddy to blow it. The day had been tough. He obviously wasn't thinking too clearly. Otherwise he would have known how close we were to turning it all around.

"Where have you been?" Nick whispered back.

"Never mind that, this is your chance!"

He just looked at me.

"To make that big impression!" I explained.

I guess Nick was a little spooked by the old place. That meant that I would have to take command.

"Look, Nick, just go up and tap on one of those windows. We'll be heroes."

Still no response.

"C'mon, Nick. Don't blow this one. Louis is already watching, so let's just give him something to look at."

Nick looked at the house, then at me, then back to the house. All my talk was obviously doing some good. If he just knocked on one of the windows, the news of his courage would quickly spread. No longer would he be "Nicholas the Dweeb," "Nicholas the Klutz," or "Nicholas the Hood." Now he could be "Nicholas the Macho." I could see it in his eyes. It all started to make sense to him.

I clucked like a chicken—just to remind him what he'd be if he didn't go. "C'mon, kid. I'll be with you all the way."

He took a deep breath and ran for the closest window—the one right above the cellar door. I let go with one of my great battle cries. "TIPPY-CANOE, I'M WITH YOU!" We were off.

In a flash Nicholas was up on the cellar doors and stretching for all he was worth to tap on the window.

This is going to be easier than I thought. That was the last thought I thought . . . before I heard the sound of cracking wood under our feet. All of a sudden the ground was missing!

We fell through the broken doors and tumbled down the cellar steps like clowns in the circus. But there was no applause. Instead there was all kinds of screeching, clawing, and squawking!

It took a moment for our eyes to adjust to the darkness. But when they did, we saw cages filled with all sorts of things that screamed and growled and gurgled.

During the fall Nicholas had dropped my sketch pad and for the moment I was trapped under it. But, not being one to panic, I calmly said, "LET'S GET OUT OF HERE!"

It did the trick. Nicholas scrambled to his feet. Unfortunately, he found himself standing face to face with large, growling teeth . . . attached to an even larger bobcat!

He let out a scream and threw himself back over a stack of wooden crates. I'd seen this kind of behavior before. I had to get him under control. I had to snap him out of it. I had to stop my teeth from chattering long enough so I could speak!

Outside, I could hear the faint sound of Louis screaming, "Get out of there, Nick. Get out of there!"

Nicholas scampered back to his feet and was ready to escape. But, before he could move, a shaft of light pierced the darkness. It came from the top of the stairs leading into the Indian's house. A huge, dark figure appeared at the door. I tried to shout, to scream, but nothing came out.

The figure began coming down the stairs . . . directly toward us!

Nick gasped. He couldn't move. He was frozen with fear.

The figure drew closer and closer. His shadow was now pouring across our faces. He was nearly on top of us.

"Nicholas!" I finally managed to squeak. "RUN!"

Nick snapped out of his trance and began looking for an escape. I was proud of the kid. With the right coaching, he could do almost anything. But what about me? I was still pinned underneath the sketch pad!

"Nicholas . . . don't leave me here!"

He jumped back and scooped up my pad . . . while I hung on for dear life.

But as he straightened up he came nose to nose with a rabbit. That's right, a poor, defenseless, rabbit. The helpless animal was hanging from the man's huge hand . . . probably his idea of an afternoon snack.

Nicholas let out a scream, tore past the big man, and raced up the stairs toward the light. We were heading right into the house. What awaited us up there was anybody's guess. But it couldn't be any worse than what awaited us in the cellar.

We were across the dimly lit room and out the front door in a flash.

We were going so fast that we hardly noticed running right into Louis on the sidewalk in front of the house. I guess he'd been waiting for our bones to be thrown out after we were eaten. We continued at light speed until we were safely in Nick's room— or, rather, his closet.

FIVE
The Lie Begins

Nicholas's head was spinning. He had just finished dinner but didn't know what he ate. His mind was too busy thinking. It's a pity, too. Because from what he could tell by the remains of the pork chops and Rice-A-Roni, it had been one of his favorite meals. Oh, well, maybe next time.

Of course his folks asked the usual first-day-at-school questions: How did he like his teacher? How were the kids? Was he making friends? You know, the usual stuff.

And, of course, Nicholas gave the usual eleven-year-old answers: Fine. OK. I guess.

It's not that he didn't want to talk to his parents. He loved talking to them. And they loved listening. No matter how busy they were, Mom and Dad always made it a point to talk with their kids.

But today he didn't feel like talking. Today, with all that Nicholas had gone through . . . well, he just wasn't sure where to start. So he wouldn't start at all. For now, the "fines," "OKs," and shrugging shoulders would just have to do.

Both parents noticed his silence. But neither of them forced him to talk. They knew he was upset about something—but they also knew they couldn't push. He would say more when he was ready.

And they were right. He would.

But now his mind was racing a billion miles an hour. It was racing about the man he'd run into. It was racing about Derrick. And it was racing about his rotten day at school.

It was racing when he finally got to sleep. . . . And it was still racing when he woke up the next morning and got ready for school.

After putting up with the usual "good-byes" and pecks on the cheek, Nicholas grabbed his stuff and headed for the door. As he opened it he couldn't help thinking, *At least today will be better than yesterday.*

But then he saw Louis. . . .

"There he is now—the man that knows no fear," Louis said. He had gathered a couple of his friends together. They had been waiting outside Nicholas's house. For how long, Nick didn't know.

"Did you get a look at him?" Louis asked.

For a moment Nick didn't know what he was talking about.

"The man, the crazy Indian—was he big?"

"Uh," Nicholas said. "Well, yeah, he . . . "

"I knew it!" Louis interrupted. "Like a monster, wasn't he?"

Again Nick was caught a little offguard. What did

Louis mean by "monster"? And why were the other kids there? And why . . . ? Then he saw it: The look on Louis's face. The boy was eager for a story. And the bigger it was the better it would be.

Nicholas wasn't sure what to do. He really didn't want to disappoint Louis—not after he had been waiting so long; not after he brought all his friends.

But, at the same time, he really didn't want to lie.

So Nicholas did the next best thing. He just didn't *disagree*. "Well, he was, uh . . . "

Louis took the bait. "I told you," he said to his friends. Then, back to Nicholas, "Were there any animals?"

"Oh, yeah, there were animals every—"

"I knew it! Did you see him eating any?"

Things were closing in on Nicholas. Up until now he didn't have to officially lie. But wasn't agreeing with a lie just as bad as telling one? And look at those kids' faces. They were so eager for a hero. Besides, all day yesterday Nick had been a real goon. And now there was a way to regain some respect!

"Well, uh," Nicholas said, hesitating. "He had a rabbit."

"HE HAD A RABBIT!? HE WAS EATING A RABBIT?"

More hesitating. "Well, it was still alive."

"He was eating a *LIVE* rabbit?!"

Uh-oh. Here it was. All Nicholas had to do was say yes. Just one little "white" lie. Who would know? Who would care? "Well, uh, I guess . . ." He stalled.

The kids continued to stare. How could he let them down? How could he let himself down?

Besides, after all he went through yesterday, he needed it. He deserved it.

"Yeah, yeah," he heard himself saying. "It was alive." And then, almost before he could catch himself, the words spilled out. "Whatever was left of it."

There, he had done it.

"This is great, man!" Louis looked like he was going to explode. "This is great!" He started running, and the other kids followed him. "Wait until they hear this. This is great!"

Nicholas waited. Part of him felt pretty good about what had happened. He was feeling good about the excitement he had caused. He was feeling good about being the center of it. After all *he* had been there. *He* was the expert. *He* was the one who had met this terrible "monster" face to face and lived to talk about it. So why shouldn't he enjoy a little glory?

But still, somewhere past the "good feelings," he felt a little guilt. Somewhere, even deeper, he knew it was wrong.

But who would know?

Who would care?

News spread faster than Nicholas could have imagined. Not only did it spread faster, it spread bigger.

In fact, by the time they got off the bus at school, he could see Louis's arms flying wildly. He was making all kinds of faces. Nicholas couldn't hear what was being said, but he did manage to catch a phrase or two about "huge claws" and "trying to catch the new kid."

That little guilt Nicholas had felt before was starting to grow.

It grew as he noticed more and more kids looking at him during class. It grew when kids stopped
talking as soon as he came near. And it grew
when complete strangers (usually girls) began
passing and saying, "Hi."

But Nicholas noticed it the most when he was
heading back from the lunch room. Not far away,
the girl with the Erector-set hair bow was telling a
crowd something about "long pointed fangs that
were dripping—" But she never finished. When
she saw Nicholas, she stopped and pointed. "There
he is now!"

Everyone in the group turned to stare.

Nicholas came to a stop. He didn't know what to
do with ten people staring at him.

He gave a weak idiotic smile (the one he had become so good at the day before).

They continued to stare.

He knew he had to say something. He knew he
had to make some sort of speech. So, he opened
his mouth and said, "Hi."

"Hi," they all said back.

Again he smiled. Being famous was tough.

They continued to stare.

He could feel his ears burning again. He glanced
around and swallowed hard. Then he started
toward the building.

The group didn't say a word. They just continued to stare.

He could feel them staring at his back as he
bumped into a couple of kids near the doorway
and finally stumbled inside.

Now he was out of sight. Now he could breathe.

But he didn't stop walking. He headed down the hall toward his classroom as quickly as possible. He could sit down there. At least for a little while, he could stay out of sight.

Now that doesn't mean Nicholas didn't enjoy the fame. To be honest, he thought it was great. But as the day went on, that "greatness" started to wear off. Instead, the good feelings started being replaced more and more by the other feeling—by that guilt.

Two-thirty had never come slower. Over and over again Nicholas looked to the clock. Over and over again he tried to make the hands move forward just by thinking. If the bell would just ring. If the day would just hurry up and end. By tomorrow everyone would forget about him and the man with the animals. By tomorrow they would find something new to talk about.

But that was tomorrow. Today was still today. And, at the moment, it didn't look like today would ever finish.

Mrs. Sanford, his teacher, was talking on and on about fractions and decimals. She kept talking and talking and talking. Then, when she was through, she talked some more. Nick kept looking at the clock. It wouldn't budge. He was beginning to believe that somehow he had managed to stumble into an episode of "The Twilight Zone" where time was always and forever frozen at 2:29.

Then it happened. The clock clicked that quarter of an inch, the bell rang, and everybody was out of their seats.

Now, at last, he could head for home. Now, at

last, he could forget about this day.

He grabbed his coat and knapsack and headed out the door, free at last—until Derrick stepped in his path.

"Hey, squid. So you're some big hero now."

Nick swallowed hard, hoping the boy wouldn't ask him to prove it.

Just then a couple of girls passed. "Hello, Nicholas."

For a second Nick was pleased. But only for a second.

"Well, I ain't buying this hero stuff," Derrick growled. "I mean what kind of fool do you take me for?"

"How many kinds are there?"

Nicholas immediately hated himself for trying to be funny with so few seconds left in his life.

But Derrick didn't laugh. He didn't get mad either. In fact, for a moment it looked as if he were actually trying to figure out the answer. But the question was too tough for him so he finally continued, "Don't try to change the subject."

Kids were starting to gather around.

"If this drooling Indian is supposed to be such a monster, eating all these pets and stuff," Derrick demanded, "then where'd you get the guts to stand up to him?"

Nicholas wasn't sure what to say. Luckily he didn't have to worry about it. Before he could open his mouth, the girl with the metal bow spoke up.

"What do you know about guts, Derrick? You're scared to even go near the place."

Nicholas could see the veins in the boy's neck

jump stand out. He could see the muscles in his jaw tighten. Finally Derrick spoke. But it wasn't loud and it wasn't boasting. It was more frightening than that. It was quiet.

And Nicholas could tell he meant every word of it. "That Indian is as good as dead."

SIX
The Plot Sickens

Nicholas doesn't remember how he got home that day. He's sure he got there eventually. And he's sure of another thing. He didn't cut through his neighbor's yard. But the exact route? Well, Nick had too many other things on his mind to pay attention to those sorts of details.

He was thinking about the whole mess. Maybe that man deserved whatever Derrick was going to do to him. After all, he was the one with the spooky, run-down house. And he was the one who caught all those poor animals and kept them locked up in cages. Maybe it was time somebody stopped him. Maybe it was time for a little justice.

Yet, Nicholas knew that Derrick Cryder was not the right one to see that justice was done. The thought made Nick more than a little nervous.

But you couldn't blame Nick. His was just a little white lie. It wasn't his fault things had gotten so out of hand. It wasn't his fault everybody kept making the story bigger. It wasn't his fault they planned to do something to the crazy man.

Or was it?

Around and around Nicholas's thoughts went until finally he arrived at home.

"Shameful, just shameful," Grandma was saying to Nick's mom as he opened the door. Grandma was at the kitchen sink cleaning lettuce. Mom was at the table snapping beans. Nicholas entered the room and made a beeline for the refrigerator.

"Hi, hon, how was school?" Mom asked.

"All right." Nick shrugged. He looked around for something to eat. He was back to his shrugs and one-word answers.

"What exactly happened?" he heard his mother ask his grandma.

"Seems some child broke into George Ravenhill's cellar yesterday—scared the poor man half to death."

Nicholas slowly came to a stop. Were they talking about him? After all, *he* had fallen through somebody's cellar yesterday.

"Is that the place," Mom asked, "a block away that's so run down?"

"Yes, it is run down," Grandma agreed. "But with his aching bones, that poor old man can barely move about."

Nicholas could feel a small knot in his stomach. They *were* talking about him *and* the crazy man. He closed the refrigerator door empty handed. Suddenly eating was the last thing he wanted to do.

Grandma continued. "Such a sweet soul, too. He takes care of all those poor injured animals."

The knot tightened.

"I don't care what his house looks like. He's the nicest man you'd ever want to meet."

More was said but Nicholas didn't hear it. All he knew was that everything the kids said and believed about that "crazy" man was wrong. Dead wrong. The house was run down because the man was crippled and couldn't keep it fixed up. The animals were in cages because he was taking care of them. And, most importantly, he was not some mean, cruel monster. He was a kind man doing his best to help others. "A sweet soul," Grandma had called him.

That knot in Nicholas's stomach continued to tighten.

He was not interested in eating now . . . and he would not be able to eat dinner later.

Nick managed to climb the stairs to his room. He closed the door and lay on his bed looking around.

At school Nick tended to be pretty quiet and shy. But you wouldn't know it by his room. It was anything but normal. All of the imagination he kept pent up when he was outside exploded when he came inside. It exploded on every wall, every shelf, every piece of furniture, the ceiling, the floor, you name it.

An automatic peanut cracker here.

A remote control pencil sharpener there.

A live goldfish swimming inside a gumball machine.

A stegosaurus lurking in the corner.

A cowboy riding the Space Shuttle.

Even a mini jukebox box that flashed "Nick's Cafe, Nick's Cafe, Nick's Cafe."

And he had only moved in a few days ago! But he had plans for turning it into a great museum full of all sorts of gizmos, widgets, and what-cha-ma-call-its. Already he had plans for:

An automatic bubble blower made from an old fan, a mannequin's head, Groucho Marx glasses, and parts of a toy lawn mower.

A voice-activated light switch.

An alarm activated by a flying puppet, a crashing jet fighter, and a swinging boxing glove.

And a robot arm attached to the ceiling that would automatically reach down and make his bed.

Of course these were all future projects. But it didn't hurt to dream. And dreaming was something Nicholas knew how to do.

Then there was his drawing table . . .

Nicholas and McGee spent hours and hours here as the boy drew one adventure after another. Of course, McGee always wanted to be the hero in the stories and Nick usually let him. But Nicholas was the one with the power. He was the one with the pencil. And, if McGee got too out of hand, Nicholas was also the one with the eraser.

But Nick wasn't sitting at his table now. Nor was he dreaming about his room. Instead, he sat on the bed and quietly drew on his sketch pad. He wasn't sure what it would be. But it slowly began looking like the face of a man.

There was a gentle tap at his door. It didn't surprise Nicholas. Getting permission to miss dinner was a major event. He knew his folks would be concerned. And he knew they'd eventually come up and talk. They were like that. And even though it was sometimes a pain, deep down inside Nicholas was glad for their concern.

He reached for his flashlight and directed its beam across the room to a toy radar dish. The dish began to swivel back and forth, switching the "Don't Walk" sign to "Walk." This triggered a miniature globe to spin above the door, which released a large sword. The sword fell, activating a series of weights and pulleys that opened the door.

Now it's true, it would have been a lot easier to just get up and open the door. But it wouldn't be nearly as inventive . . . or as much fun.

"Can I come in?" Dad poked his head around the door.

Nick nodded.

The man entered and glanced about the room. "Sure fixing this place up in a hurry," he commented.

It was true, and Nicholas was pleased his dad noticed. But for now he just shrugged it off.

"Missed you at dinner."

More silence. The boy knew what his father was doing. The man wanted to talk. But Nicholas didn't know what to say. Part of him wanted Dad to stick around. The other part wanted him to go away.

Dad sensed the confusion. So, instead of pushing and asking a lot of hard questions, he just quietly walked over to the other end of the room. "You know, living here with Grandma is going to be great. I've got a lot of memories about this old place."

To be honest, Nicholas felt he'd already had enough memories.

"It was right over there your Uncle Rob 'accidentally' shoved me into the dresser and chipped this tooth. Oh, how I cried. I almost got him thrown in jail." Dad smiled at the memory.

Nicholas tried to join in with a smile of his own. But he didn't have much success.

More silence.

Finally Dad strolled over to the foot of the bed and sat. Then, after a long moment, he spoke. "What's up, Nick?"

"About what?" The words were out of the boy's mouth before he could stop them. But they did no good. He knew that his Dad knew. Maybe not the details, but they'd been friends too many years for him to be able to hide something this important.

Finally, Nicholas answered. "I don't know." He stalled, giving his Dad one last chance to give up and leave. But his Dad had all the time in the world. He wasn't going anywhere and Nicholas knew it.

Finally, seeing no way out, Nick began. "What if— what if you said something about somebody and, you know, they got in real trouble for it?"

A trace of relief started to cross Dad's face. "Well, son, nobody likes to get somebody in trouble. But if it's the truth and—"

Nicholas's eyes shot down.

Dad didn't miss it.

"Of course," he continued gently, "if it's not the truth . . ."

Nicholas didn't say a word.

52

His dad finally saw the picture. His son had lied. With that information he quietly continued. "Then a lot of people could get hurt."

Nicholas still didn't look up. But that was OK. He didn't need to. Dad knew what was going on in his mind and he wanted to help. So he gently went on. "Of course, there's the person that's being lied about. But there's also the person who's doing the lying."

Nick looked up. It's true, *he* was hurting. Sure, he may be causing that old man some problems. But he, Nicholas Martin, was also hurting—more than he thought possible.

Dad continued. "I mean, not only will the truth

eventually find the liar out, but the very fact that lying is a sin—well that sin starts cutting off that person's friendship with God."

Of course! That's what he'd been feeling! The knot in his stomach, that feeling. Sure it felt great to be the hero, to have everyone think you were a hotshot. But that other feeling—that feeling of guilt. That's what it was. It was cutting off his friendship with God, with Jesus. It was sin. Plain and simple. And it hurt.

Still, Dad was not finished. "But you know there's a third person that gets hurt."

A frown crossed Nicholas's face. There was more? Wasn't the pain and ache enough?

"Yes," Dad continued, "there is one more person who gets hurt."

Nicholas waited.

"Remember, Jesus said that whatever we do for others we do for him."

Nicholas nodded. He remembered hearing something like that in Sunday school.

"Well, that being the case, it stands to reason that whatever we do to others we do to him. If you lie and hurt another person, you're actually lying to Jesus and hurting him."

Nicholas was stunned. He had no idea that such a little lie could cause such big problems. But his dad was right. He could see it clearly now. Not only was he hurting the old man, not only was he hurting himself, he was also hurting Jesus. Everything he said, everything he did against that man was also against Jesus.

The knot in his stomach was very painful. And

now he could also feel a lump in his throat. This isn't what he wanted. He just wanted the kids to like him, to look up to him. He didn't want this. But how could he stop it? How could he fix it?

He tried to speak. His voice was thick and raspy, barely above a whisper. "What do I do?"

His dad waited a long moment as Nicholas looked to him for help. Finally, his father spoke. It wasn't a mean answer. But it wasn't a simple answer either. Instead, he asked just one question: "What do you think?"

SEVEN
The Attack

The alley was dark and full of shadows. There were a few back porch lights on. But the fog was so thick that the lights barely shown. Everything was very, very still. Dark and still. Then a porch light flickered on, lighting the face of Derrick Cryder. He quickly moved back into the shadows and continued to wait.

Nicholas was in his room sketching again. His dad had left several minutes before. Now all he could do was sketch and think. What his dad said kept echoing inside his mind. *"Whatever you do to others, you're doing to Jesus."*

The drawing was definitely taking on the face of a person. Nicholas was shading in the nose now. It was a strong nose, a noble nose.

Derrick was standing along the wire fence. He blew into his hands and stomped his feet slightly. The fog had brought a chill to the night.

There was the scratch of gravel off in the distance. He spun around just in time to see one of his fellow gang members appear.

"Hey, man, what's happening?" he whispered. "Soon as the others show up, let's get rolling."

They huddled together just out of the light. And they continued to wait.

Nicholas was working on the chin now. Like the nose, it was going to be a strong chin. *Whisk, whisk, whisk*—his pencil seemed to be moving faster than normal as he continued shading. And Nicholas's own face? The boy had never been in such deep thought. And still he continued to draw.

"Whatever you do to others, you're doing to Jesus."

"All right, there they are!" Derrick whispered.

Two other kids appeared in the alley. Big kids. Kids looking for trouble. They arrived and exchanged hand slaps and more street jive.

"All right. Let's do it to it!"

"Yeah."

"Let's show that Indian!" *BANG.* Derrick slammed the wire fence hard, causing it to rattle. A distant dog started barking, followed by another. But that didn't matter. Derrick and the guys were moving out. Derrick and the guys were ready for action.

They started down the alley. Four of them. Their faces appearing and disappearing in the shadows. No one said a word. No one had to. They knew what they had to do and nothing would stop them.

Now Nicholas was working on the eyes. They were thoughtful eyes, haunting eyes. Eyes full of pain. Eyes full of sorrow. In fact, if you were to have looked into Nicholas's own eyes at that exact moment you would have seen the very same look— thoughtful, painful, sorrowful. The boy was not crying, not yet. But, like the sketch, he was definitely aching.

He hesitated a moment. The eyes were finished. So was the nose, the chin, the hair. But something was missing. Something still was not right. Then he saw it. In a flash he took the pencil and made a fierce, strong line across the forehead. And then another in the opposite direction. For a moment it looked like he had made a giant X across the top of the head. But he was not finished. He made another slash, and one across it, making another X. And then another.

His eyes began to fill with tears. He angrily brushed them aside and continued to draw.

Derrick and his gang came out of the alley and into the bright street lights. They didn't care if anyone saw them now. They no longer needed the darkness. There were four of them and four could do just about whatever they wanted.

The old man's house was just ahead.

Derrick scooped up a large rock. His buddies did likewise. And, after a few more steps, they were in front of the house.

There was only one light on. It was downstairs. But it was good enough.

Derrick leaned back and let his rock fly. . . .

It was a quiet evening inside George Ravenhill's living room. He had put on some gentle music and was enjoying the fire in the fireplace. For several hours he had been hovering over the work table. That afternoon a young cardinal had flown into one of the neighbor's picture windows. The neighbor had brought it over and he was doing all he could to save it. At the moment he was trying to feed it some sugar water with an eye dropper. It was hard trying to pick up the eye dropper with his crippled hands. But at last he succeeded.

Suddenly, there was a loud *CRASH*!

Ravenhill spun around just in time to see the rock fly into the room. It was followed by a thousand bits of glass. He covered his eyes with his arm just in time as the glass sprayed over him.

There was laughter outside but he didn't have time to see who it was.

Another rock came crashing through the window followed by more glass. Quickly, he grabbed a nearby towel and threw it over the cardinal. Glass was flying in all directions but he was more concerned about the bird's safety than his own. There was one more *CRASH* and then all was silent.

Well, not really silent. Outside on the porch, some of the other caged animals he was taking care of were scared—dogs, birds, kittens, his pet rabbit, even a raccoon. They were barking, and screaming, and crying.

Ravenhill was also frightened. He lay huddled on the floor shaking like a leaf. What had he done? Why were people trying to hurt him?

Time passed slowly but there were no more

rocks. Finally he rose to his feet and hobbled across the broken glass to stand beside the shattered window. After a deep breath he pushed the curtains aside to look out. But there was no sign of movement. Everything was quiet again.

Except for the animals. They were still very frightened and it would take a long time to quiet them down. But the animals were not the only ones afraid.

George Ravenhill would not be able to sleep that night.

Nor would Nicholas. Oh, he was in his bed all right. His eyes were shut. In fact, he even managed to doze off once in a while. But each time he fell asleep the dreams would come. Bad dreams. Scary dreams. Sometimes they were monsters, sometimes demons. Sometimes he was just falling and falling and falling. But each and every time he would wake from them with a start. And, after convincing himself that it was just a dream, he would close his eyes and drift back off to sleep. But it would be only for a few minutes. Another dream would soon be coming.

Not far away was the picture Nick had been drawing. It was finished now. And now, with its noble nose, strong chin, and deep, sorrowful eyes, there was no missing who it was. It was a portrait of Jesus.

But this was not a smiling Jesus. This was not the happy Jesus with arms reaching out that Nick always saw at Sunday school. This was a different Jesus. This was a Jesus who was hurting.

And, on top of his head were the *Xs* Nicholas had drawn. But they were not just *Xs*. Strung together they had become a crown of thorns. The crown of thorns Jesus had been forced to wear. The crown of thorns the soldiers had jammed down hard on his head until it bled. The crown of thorns he had worn as he died on the cross for all of our sins.

"Whatever you do to others, you're doing to Jesus."

EIGHT
A Time for Action

Nicholas was right—and he was wrong.

He was right when he figured the kids at school would forget about him by the next day. It's true, he was no longer in the spotlight. They were treating him just like your average kid.

But he was wrong when he thought they'd forget about the old man. Derrick saw to that. Now Derrick was the one with all the courage. He was the one who attacked the house. He was the one who actually stood up to the "monster." Nick may have fallen through his cellar doors. But Derrick was the one who taught the man a lesson. Derrick Cryder was the hero for today.

And Derrick played it for all it was worth.

He played it at recess when the shy girls looked at him—or when the bolder ones actually came up and flirted.

He played it at lunchtime when the guys came up and slapped him on the back.

He was enjoying the attention so much that he

didn't want it to end. So, by the end of the day, he was making new plans. He was going to continue being the hero. "Trash the Indian's House, Part II" was about to begin.

But Nicholas didn't know that. Not yet. And that was probably good. You see, the day had been rough enough on him as it was. Because each time he heard what Derrick had done, a pain shot through him—that pain in his stomach.

It's true that Nicholas was not the one who broke the windows. But a part of him felt as though he was the one. Derrick may have thrown the rocks, but Nicholas was the one who started the lie. Nick was the one who let it grow. And Nick was the one who stood by and let everyone believe it.

Nicholas was sitting in math class when the 2:30 bell rang to signal the end of the day. Everyone sprang into action. They began packing up their knapsacks and grabbing their coats. They began heading for home. But Nicholas stayed behind at his desk. He was drawing some little design on his sketchpad when Louis suddenly popped his head into the room.

"Hey Nick! If you don't move it, you're going to miss the action!"

"What action?" Nick asked.

"Derrick and his friends are going to put the finishing touches on the old Indian!"

Nick couldn't believe his ears. They were going back. They were going back to Mr. Ravenhill's to do more damage!

Louis flashed him a grin. "Should be good," he said. And he was out the door.

Now Nicholas was all alone.

What should he do?

What could he do?

This was a time for Major Mishap to spring into action! Not only for the sake of poor Mr. Ravenhill, but also for my little pal, Nick. He just didn't know what to do. So, dashing into a nearby sketchpad, I changed into my super-hero clothes. I leaped from the pad in Nick's knapsack and out onto the top of his desk.

"This is it, loyal friend," I declared, as my cape blew behind me in the wind.

"McGee, please, not Major Mishap again."

Nick sounded a bit upset. Now, most wrongdoers respond that way when Major Mishap arrives on the scene. But it seemed a bit strange coming from my own partner. Now I admit some of my adventures haven't always come out exactly perfect, but this was no time to be picky about the past. . . .

"It's time to right the wrongs, to restore justice to its rightful place, to—"

"McGee," he interrupted. "If I try to stop those guys they'll kill me!"

Over the years Nick and I have been through a lot together. And, although most of our times are fun and games, I know when he's hurting. And this . . . well, this was one of those times. We looked at each other for a long moment, searching for an answer. And then, quietly, I said what we both knew.

"There isn't much time, kid."

His lips tightened for a second. Then suddenly, without a word, he jumped to his feet. Grabbing his jacket with one hand, he snatched up the knapsack with the other—so quickly that I barely had time to leap back inside.

Wheeling toward the exit, he raced out the door.

We were on our way to George Ravenhill's to save the day . . . or die trying.

The balloon exploded against the side of Ravenhill's house. It was full of paint. Red paint. Red paint that left an ugly stain as it ran down the side of the wall.

Derrick and the guys were out on the sidewalk. Laughing. Cheering. Jeering. Their hands were full of balloons. Their hearts were full of hate. "Come on," Derrick called. "Come on out!"

He leaned back and fired another balloon at the house.

SPLAT!

This one was blue—and equally as ugly.

Not to be outdone, the rest of the boys started to join in, throwing their balloons as hard as they could.

SPLAT . . . SPLAT, SPLAT . . . SPLAT.

Red, yellow, blue—balloon after balloon exploded against the house.

The animals on the porch began to panic. They paced back and forth in their cages. They screamed. They howled. They barked crazily.

But there was no movement inside that house.

"What's the matter, Indian?" one of the guys yelled. "Afraid of somebody that can fight back?"

There was no movement inside the house because Mr. Ravenhill was frozen in fear. He had flattened himself against the far wall. This was the second attack in two days. He had no idea what was happening—or why. All he knew was that somebody out there meant business. And he knew that if they really wanted to, those somebodies could hurt his animals and destroy his home.

And there was nothing he could do about it.

The buses were one yellow blur as Nicholas raced past them. He was running for all he was worth. Somebody had to stop Derrick. Somebody had to put an end to all of these lies. Nick wasn't sure how he'd do it—but he knew he had to try.

"Come on out, creep! Let's go, chicken!"

SPLAT, SPLAT . . . SPLAT.

The boys shouted and threw more balloons.

The animals cried and howled in panic.

Finally Derrick had worked up enough courage to break from the boys and head toward the porch. "I'll show that bum. . . . "

For a moment the other kids held back. But as Derrick flew up the porch steps, they also found their courage and followed. "Yeah, let's get him— let's show that Indian!"

Nicholas was still running. He was only a few blocks away but his throat felt like it was on fire. He was breathing too hard. The autumn air was so cold that it seemed to cut a deep groove into the back of his throat. But he kept running.

Derrick was on the porch now. He had ripped off the door to one of the little pigeon cages and was holding the cage high over his head. The birds flew out as quickly as they could. *CRASH!* The boy threw the cage down on the porch and laughed as it splintered into a million pieces.

The other kids followed his lead. They pushed over every cage they could find. They ripped open every door that could be opened. Frightened and panicky animals scurried in all directions. And, once the cages were emptied, those cages were smashed into pieces on the porch. One after another after another.

It was a nightmare full of crying animals, broken cages, and laughing boys.

Nick felt it in his legs now—or rather, didn't feel it. His thighs and calves had started to feel like rubber. But he continued to run, pumping as hard as he could.

He turned to cut across the street when he suddenly heard the screech of brakes. He looked up just in time to see a car skid to a stop. It was less than five feet from him.

The driver looked as white as a sheet and started to shout something. But Nicholas didn't have time for chit-chat. He was off again.

He finally flew around the last corner and saw the old man's house just ahead. But what he saw slowly brought him to a stop.

In front of him was the porch—or what was left of it. Everywhere there were broken and overturned tables, cages shattered and destroyed. And paint—lots of blue, yellow, and red paint—dripping everywhere on the porch, the walls, the steps.

Pleased with their work, Derrick and his friends turned and started to leave. They headed down the steps and didn't even see Nicholas until they were right in front of him. But, as always, Derrick had the right word for the right occasion. "Now who's the hero, squid?"

And, before Nicholas could answer, the boy took off down the street with the rest of his friends. Everyone was laughing and shouting over the victory.

Nicholas watched as they disappeared. Then, slowly, he turned back to the house.

He couldn't believe his eyes. It was awful—like seeing those TV pictures of what a tornado leaves behind. Terrible.

And then Nicholas saw it—or rather, he heard it. Some sort of movement on the porch. Some sort of sound.

Slowly, the boy started toward the porch. He saw more and more damage as he got closer. And then he saw George Ravenhill.

Somehow the man had hobbled onto the porch. But now, he was on his knees. In his arms he was holding the rabbit. The very same rabbit Nicholas had seen in the cellar. Only it didn't look exactly the same. Now it looked very limp. And, as Ravenhill continued to hold the tiny creature, Nicholas noticed something else. A small trickle of blood was running from its nose across the big man's hand.

Ravenhill heard Nicholas and looked up. For the

first time since the cellar their eyes met.

Nicholas gasped.

He didn't gasp because of the sadness on the old man's face. He didn't gasp because of the tear that was slowly moving across the old man's cheek.

Nicholas gasped because of his eyes. They were the same eyes he had drawn the night before. They were the eyes of Christ—the sorrowful eyes— the eyes full of such love and pain.

And, once again, Nicholas heard his Dad's haunting words.

"Whatever you to do others, you're doing to Jesus."

NINE
Wrapping Up

That evening Nicholas and his dad sat in George
Ravenhill's living room. The old man listened quietly as the boy explained all that had happened.
There were lots of tears and lots of apologies. But,
somehow everyone knew that was not enough. A
lot of damage had happened because of Nicholas's
lie. A lot of suffering. And to think it could all be
forgotten with a simple "I'm sorry"—well that just
was not enough.

So . . . the following Saturday, at the crack of
dawn, Nicholas was on George Ravenhill's porch
scrubbing off paint, fixing cages, and sweeping . . .
lots and lots of sweeping.

Nicholas knew that he was forgiven. That was
the beauty of being a Christian. If you mess up, no
matter how bad, God will forgive you if you just
ask. Plain and simple. That's why Jesus died on
the cross—to take the punishment for whatever
we do wrong.

Of course, you have to be serious when you ask

him to forgive you. Nicholas was serious. So, as far as God was concerned, the boy was perfectly innocent. It was as if he had never sinned. Not a bad deal.

But there was still the mess and there was still the hurt he had caused Mr. Ravenhill.

So, Nicholas was sweeping and sweeping . . . and sweeping.

He was still sweeping when Louis appeared.

"You really didn't see any of that stuff you said, did you?" Louis asked.

"No," Nicholas admitted. "I didn't see a thing."

"Man—" Louis shook his head. "I wouldn't want to be in your shoes Monday. You're going to catch it good."

Nicholas had to nod. It was one thing to be forgiven by God. But quite another to face the other kids. "I should have told the truth" was all he could say.

"Well, it was fun while it lasted" was all Louis could say. Then, after a moment, he got up and walked off.

If anyone knows what fun is, it's me. And the last few days didn't fit into my definition of fun. But, not wanting to dwell on the past, I was determined to make the most of what we'd been through. So, as Nick continued to sweep, I sat near one of the animal's watering trays. It belonged to the raccoon—kind of a nice critter if you didn't smell his breath.

"This is real good," I said to Nick, trying to offer

encouragement. "I mean us helping like this. Yes, sir. Uh, you missed a spot."

Nick gave me a look.

"What?" I said.

He just shook his head. Finally, after a couple of moments, he spoke. "I really can't make up for what I did, McGee. I mean, I know God's forgiven me and stuff, but . . . I don't know."

Just then Mr. Ravenhill stepped out onto the front porch. In one hand he was holding the rabbit. With all the bandages it looked a little like a mummy, but it did look like it would get better. In the other hand he held a glass of lemonade. It looked good since it was so hot outside.

"When you're through here," he said gruffly, "you can start working on the cellar steps."

"Yes, sir," Nick said.

"Oh, and uh . . . here." Mr. Ravenhill set the lemonade he had been carrying on a nearby barrel. As he hobbled back into the house, he also offered the kid a trace of a smile.

I've got to tell you, lemonade might hit the spot when it comes to thirst. But what really hit the spot for Nick was that smile. It sent a message that we would remember for a long time. Knowing that the man had forgiven us made all the difference in the world.

"You know, McGee," Nick mused, "saying you're sorry is one thing, but to actually do something. . . . Well, it's like Dad said, it's good for Mr. Ravenhill— and it's good for me."

"You?" I said, slipping into the raccoon's water

dish for a little dip. (I figured a few laps around the pool would be good for me.)

"It reminds me . . . ," Nick continued. "It reminds me how much sin—even a little one—really hurts."

Usually I'm not at a loss for words, but this time there was nothing I could add to what he had said. He was absolutely right.

A moment later the raccoon decided to play with me in his pool. Who knows, maybe I reminded him of his rubber ducky. In any case, he wanted to play patty-cake. And since it was his pool, I went along with it.

"Easy boy, that tickles . . . hee, hee," I giggled as the masked animal played with me.

"McGee," Nicholas said, "why don't you do something to help?"

It seemed to me I'd been helping quite a bit these last few days. Anyway, whipping out my scrub brush and shower cap, I figured I'd make the most out of my dip in the dish.

"I'd love to, but the Lone Ranger here's offered to help me take a bath."

"Sure," Nick said. "They always wash their food before they eat it."

"Right-o," I said. "They always wash their—" and then it hit me—"FOOD?! NICHOLAS!"

The kid broke out laughing. I couldn't believe it. I was about to become the soup of the day, and Nick just kept grinning like a cat in a room full of mice. And to make matters worse, the crazy raccoon was getting rougher by the minute.

"Nick! You've got to get me out of here!" The animal pushed me hard under the water. I came up

coughing and choking. "Blub . . . bup . . . oooff . . .
NICHOLAS?!" And down I went again.

What an awful way to go.

"All right, all right." Nick was laughing. "You're
such a scaredy cat." He lifted the raccoon from the
bowl.

"Nicholas . . . ," I gasped, clinging to the edge of
the bowl.

"Some animals have no taste," he joked as he set
the large animal to the ground.

"Very funny, ho-ho, that's real funny," I panted.
"You should be in the circus—as a clown, you
Bozo!"

He threw me a grin. And, as mad as I was, I
couldn't help smiling back. We'd made it through
another adventure. A little worse for wear, but a
little better off. And it had happened all because of
one sin. No wonder God hates sin so much.

Anyway, things were finally getting back to normal. And that was good. But knowing Nick—and
knowing me—normal wouldn't stay normal for
long. I was sure there was another adventure waiting . . . just around the corner.